# The Little Engine That Could™

## VALENTINE'S DAY SURPRISE!

Platt & Munk, Publishers

Copyright © 2003 by Platt & Munk, Publishers. All rights reserved. Published by Platt & Munk, Publishers, a division of Grosset & Dunlap, which is a division of Penguin Young Readers Group, 345 Hudson Street, New York, New York 10014. THE LITTLE ENGINE THAT COULD, engine design, and "I THINK I CAN" are trademarks of Penguin Group (USA) Inc. Registered in U.S. Patent and Trademark Office. Printed in the U.S.A.

*Library of Congress Cataloging-in-Publication Data is available.*

ISBN 0-448-43280-3     A B C D E F G H I J

# The Little Engine That Could™

## VALENTINE'S DAY SURPRISE!

written by Monique Z. Stephens
based on the original story by Watty Piper
illustrated by Cristina Ong

Platt & Munk, Publishers

It was a special day at the Piney Vale
Train Station—Valentine's Day!

The Little Engine That Could smiled to see passengers being surprised by friends and family bringing them flowers and candy. Even the station workers and train conductors were smiling and exchanging valentines.

"What pretty valentines!" the Little Engine That Could said to herself. She wondered what it would be like to receive a valentine made just for her.

Mr. John, the manager of the Piney Vale Train Station, walked up to the Little Blue Engine. "Hi, Little Blue! Happy Valentine's Day!"

"It *is* a happy day, isn't it?" said the Little Blue Engine. "It's so nice to see so many people showing their love for one another!"

"Well, soon, today is going to get even better," said Mr. John. "After all, today's the day that Lucy Locomotive, Choo Choo Charlie, and Engine Eddie come to Piney Vale Train Station!"

"That's right!" the Little Engine That Could said happily.

Lucy Locomotive, Choo Choo Charlie, and Engine Eddie were her friends from Maple Falls, a small town nearby. Their train station was closing, so they were moving to Piney Vale.

Waiting for her friends to arrive, the Little Engine That Could was nearly ready to burst with excitement.

At last she spotted the three trains chugging toward her on the tracks. She blew her whistle long and hard. They were finally here!

"Hi there, Little Blue!" Engine Eddie said in his deep, booming voice.

"I can't believe we're all going to be living in Piney Vale together!" Lucy Locomotive said excitedly.

"Little Blue, Little Blue!" Choo Choo Charlie piped up. "Isn't it going to be fun? We'll see one another every day and we can talk and play games and tell jokes and have parties all the time!"

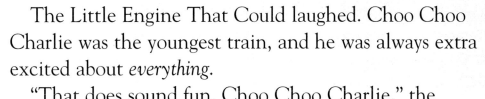

The Little Engine That Could laughed. Choo Choo Charlie was the youngest train, and he was always extra excited about *everything*.

"That does sound fun, Choo Choo Charlie," the Little Blue Engine said. "Hey, why don't we have a party today? It *is* Valentine's Day, after all—and your first day at Piney Vale! We should celebrate!"

"Oh, can we, Engine Eddie? What do you say, Lucy? Pleeease?" Choo Choo Charlie begged.

Before Lucy Locomotive and Engine Eddie could reply, Mr. John spoke up.

"That's a great idea, Little Blue, but I'm afraid there's no time for a party today. I have to show the new trains around and give them their schedules so they'll be ready for their routes tomorrow," said Mr. John. "Also, I really need you to run some important errands."

The Little Engine That Could couldn't help but feel a little disappointed.

"Don't feel bad, Little Blue," said Lucy Locomotive.
"We'll still be here when you get back. Maybe we can have
a party next weekend instead!"

The Little Blue Engine smiled. "That's true," she replied.

"And I've got a joke for you before you go," said
Choo Choo Charlie. "Wanna hear it?"

"Sure," said the Little Blue Engine.

"Okay. How can you tell when a train is gone?"
Choo Choo Charlie asked.

The Little Engine That Could thought for a moment.
"I don't know. How?"

"It leaves its tracks behind!" Choo Choo Charlie said gleefully.

The Little Blue Engine laughed as she started up her engines
and rolled down the tracks.

The Little Engine That Could had
to run a lot of errands for Mr. John.
She made a visit to the post office
to send out some packages.

She went to the print shop to pick up a batch of train schedules.

She stopped at the grocery store for a box of goodies
to fill the drink and snack machines in the train station.

And then she picked up the week's
supply of coal—her last errand for the day!

The Little Engine That Could was happy to be on her way back to the train station. She couldn't wait to talk more with her friends!

Chugging along the rails toward home, the Little Blue
Engine passed Mrs. Lee, the mail carrier. The train tooted
her horn in greeting. Mrs. Lee smiled and waved back.

The lacy red-and-white valentine in her hand was the
prettiest valentine the Little Engine That Could had ever
seen. She sighed, feeling a little sad that she didn't have a
special valentine, too.

As she got closer to the train station, the Little Engine That Could spotted something unusual hovering in the sky. It was a ring of smoke—and it was shaped like a heart!

Curious, the Little Engine That Could pushed herself faster.
When she rounded the bend approaching Piney Vale Train
Station, the heart came closer into view. Now she could read
the words inside of it: HAPPY VALENTINE'S DAY!

When she rolled into the station, all of her friends were
standing there. "Surprise!" they all yelled.

The Little Engine That Could gasped. "For me?" she asked. "I've never heard of a surprise Valentine's Day party before!"

Mr. John laughed. "Neither had we, until now! But I and everyone else wanted to do something to let you know how much we appreciate you for all your hard work around here— and how much we love you for being such a good friend!"

The Little Blue Engine blushed.

"We wanted it to be a surprise," Mr. John explained. "That's why I sent you on all those errands!"

"That's also why he told you that we new trains had so much stuff to learn around here," said Lucy Locomotive. "So you'd really believe we were all too busy to celebrate!"

"But we didn't let Choo Choo Charlie in on our little secret," Engine Eddie said. "We waited until *after* you left to let Charlie know what was going on. Sometimes it's hard for him to keep a secret!" Engine Eddie laughed heartily and Choo Choo Charlie joined in.

"That's true," he said sheepishly. "I get too excited and I forget. But it was *my* idea to draw your valentine across the sky using puffs of smoke! Do you like it, Little Blue? Do you?" Choo Choo Charlie asked anxiously.

The Little Blue Engine gazed up at her very own personal valentine hovering above them in the air. She smiled at Charlie.

"It's the most perfect valentine a train could ever wish for," she said happily. "I love it—and I love all of you. Happy Valentine's Day, everyone!"

And it was!